Hello World

*To my mother, who showed
me the world ~ M. F.*

First U.S. edition 2003

Library of Congress Cataloging-in-Publication Data is available.

Library of Congress Catalog Card Number 2002073948

ISBN 0-7636-2112-9

2 4 6 8 10 9 7 5 3

Printed in China

This book was typeset in Calligraphic Bold.
The illustrations were done in watercolor, pastel, and colored pencil.

Candlewick Press, 2067 Massachusetts Avenue, Cambridge, Massachusetts 02140

visit us at www.candlewick.com

Hello World

Michael Foreman

CANDLEWICK PRESS
CAMBRIDGE, MASSACHUSETTS

"Wake up, Baby. Let's go and see the world."

"Listen. The birds are singing,
'Wake up, wake up.'"

"Hello, kittens. Come and see the world with us."

Will there be
trees to climb?

"Yes, and much, much more."

"Hello, puppies.
Come and see the world."

Will there be fields to run in?

"Yes, run along
with us."

"Hello, Mrs. Frog. We're off to see the world."

Will there be a warm rock to rest on?

"Yes, come and see."

"Hello, Mrs. Duck. We're off to see the world."

Will there be a pond for me and my ducklings?

"Yes, a pond and more besides."

We'll waddle along with you, then.

"Hello, Mrs. Hen. Come with us and see the world."

Will there be wheat to peck?

"Yes, come and bring your chicks."

"Follow us, follow us;
  we're off to see the world."

And they saw a pond
with warm rocks to rest on.

And they saw
trees to climb.

And they saw fields of flowers and wheat.

And they loved it all.

Is there more?

"Yes, come and see."

And together they climbed the hill.

and saw the moon

And they looked up

When they reached the top,
they sat and looked, and all the
wide world was before them.

It was wonderful.

looking back at them.

and the stars